I0079943

Seasons Change

A Story About Dealing with Grief & Loss

DWANETTA BEAVER REED

Copyright© 2024 by Dwanetta Beaver Reed
All rights reserved. This book or any portion thereof may not be reproduced or used in any manner whatsoever without the express written permission of the publisher except for the use of brief quotations in a book review.

Limits of Liability and Disclaimer of Warranty

The author and publisher shall not be liable for your misuse of this material. This book is strictly for informational purposes. The purpose of this book is to educate. The author and publisher do not guarantee anyone following these techniques, suggestions, tips, ideas, or strategies will become successful. The author and publisher shall have neither liability nor responsibility to anyone with respect to any loss or damage caused, or alleged to be caused, directly or indirectly by the information contained in this book. Views expressed in this publication do not necessarily reflect the views of the publisher.

Printed in the United States of America
Keen Vision Publishing, LLC
www.publishwithkvp.com
ISBN: 978-1-955316-59-0

In loving memory of my daughter,
Katherine.

A Message to Parents & Guardians

Grief and loss are not happy topics to discuss, but unfortunately, they are experiences we cannot avoid. Tools, resources, and conversations surrounding grief and loss are necessary to help us navigate the challenges those experiences create. Loss covers a wide spectrum of circumstances, and this book, in particular, addresses the emotional whirlwind we experience when we lose loved ones.

When I was a child, I experienced the loss of relatives, but nothing prepared me for the year 2018. My seven-year-old daughter, Katherine, passed away, and my family and I were devastated. She left behind her five-year-old brother, Lawrence IV, and a sister, Destiny, whom she asked for but never got to meet. From that loss emerged this book.

It has been a journey to watch our son navigate through his grief, and my husband and I made some mistakes along the way. Some parts of the story are similar to what occurred during that particular month of May. We are thankful for licensed therapists (which I am not) who provided excellent tools to allow for better processing of loss and ways to cope. I hope this book reaches your child and helps them find their path to healing.

As adults, we often have an intimate, though undesired, relationship with grief and loss. Through life, we've learned to, at the very least, expect it to happen. Even if our methods may not be healthy, we've figured out some way to approach grief and loss. For children, grief and loss can be very confusing, frustrating, and overwhelming. Very often, they don't understand what's happening. Sometimes, as parents and guardians, we are so overwhelmed in our own grieving process that it may be easy to forget children are navigating through the same loss, too. Therefore, this book has a dual purpose.

- To help children understand the emotions that come with loss and grief, and give parents and guardians a tool to use as a conversation starter to discuss the thoughts, feelings, and emotions children may be experiencing.
- To encourage adults to also feel their feelings and find healthier ways to navigate the challenges of grief and loss.

Again, I am not a therapist, but I offer this book to you and your family as one who intimately understands the grief journey. I pray this book helps you, your children, and your family find a path to healing. I encourage you and your children to express your emotions healthily together. That is where healing begins.

Dwanetta Beaver Reed

One crisp Fall morning, Devin ran to catch the bus for school with his best friend, Savannah. The leaves, once green, were now red, yellow, and orange. Devin smiled as he imagined the fun he and Savannah would have raking the leaves once they fell to the ground.

Savannah had been absent from school for a few days. Devin had really missed his friend. "Hurry up, slowpoke! I'm going to get to the bus stop before you," Devin yelled when he saw Savannah walking down the sidewalk.

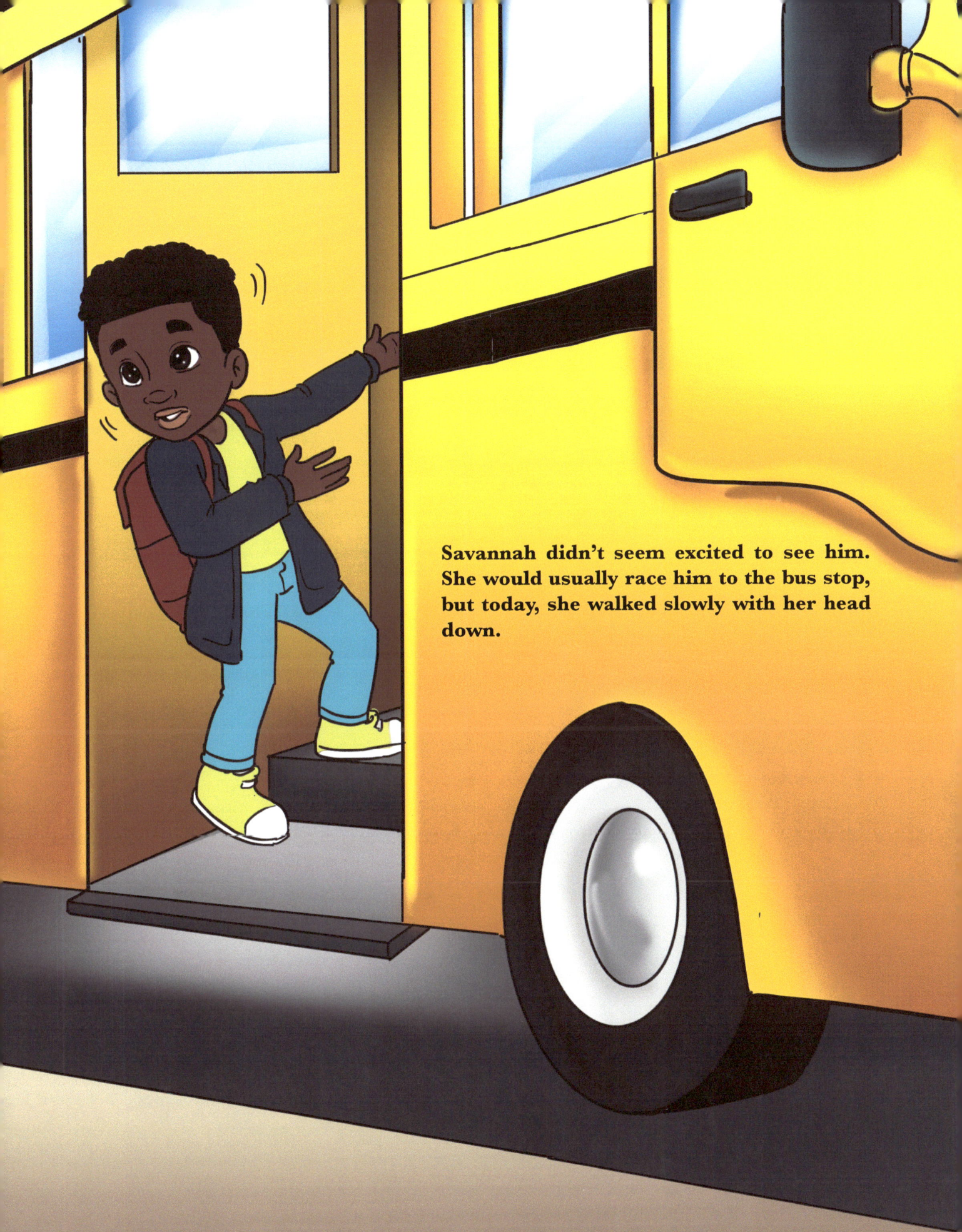

Savannah didn't seem excited to see him. She would usually race him to the bus stop, but today, she walked slowly with her head down.

Once seated in their favorite middle seats, Devin looked at Savannah and waited for her to share a new historical fact she had learned over the weekend. But Savannah sat quietly.

Devin was very confused. He didn't know what was wrong with Savannah. They usually talked and laughed the entire ride to school. Devin wanted to talk about everything with Savannah like they always did, but Savannah didn't say anything.

"Are you okay?" He finally asked.
Savannah shrugged and looked out of the window sadly.
"Where have you been? Did your mom take you to school?" Devin asked.

Savannah shrugged and continued to look out of the window.
"Did you do something cool this weekend?" Devin asked, eager to talk to his friend about something.
Savannah shook her head no.

Devin could tell something was wrong with his friend, but he did not know what to say to make her feel better. So he remained silent for the rest of the bus ride.

When they got to school, Savannah still didn't say anything. They just walked into school in silence. All day in class, Devin worried about Savannah.

When he got on the bus, Devin anxiously waited for Savannah to sit next to him. He saw her walking his way and was thrilled that Savannah appeared happier.

"Want to share my cookies from lunch?" Savannah asked him when she sat down. "They're your favorite: Chocolate chip!"

"Sure!" Devin said. He was happy that his friend was doing better. He didn't want to make her sad again, so he didn't talk about how strange Savannah acted that morning.

The two friends talked and ate cookies all the way home. Savannah even raced Devin to their neighborhood. Even though she seemed okay, Devin noticed something was different about his friend. Some days, she was the same old Savannah. Other days, she seemed sad and very quiet.

One day after school, Devin asked his mother what she thought was happening with Savannah.

"Everyone has up and down days sometimes," Devin's mom told him. "Some days, we will be very happy. Other days, we may feel sad about things in our lives. Give Savannah a little time. Everything will be okay."

Devin took his mother's advice and gave Savannah space. When Savannah was quiet, Devin sat quietly with his friend. He didn't ask questions. He didn't force her to be happy. He allowed Savannah to be however she wanted.

After several weeks, Savannah was better and back to her normal self. When all the leaves had fallen off the trees, Devin and Savannah raked them and jumped into the piles before finally bagging them. Devin was so happy Savannah got better. Raking the leaves wouldn't have been as fun without her.

Soon, it was winter, and school closed for the holidays and winter break. Devin knew he and Savannah wouldn't see each other as often because Savannah and her family traveled south for the holidays.

The holiday season was always a fun time for Devin's family. Devin couldn't wait for all the fun activities his family had planned.

When Devin came home from school, his grandad was sleeping in the guest room at his house. Devin's parents told him that Grandad had gotten sick and would live with them for a while. Devin and his parents would help Grandad get better.

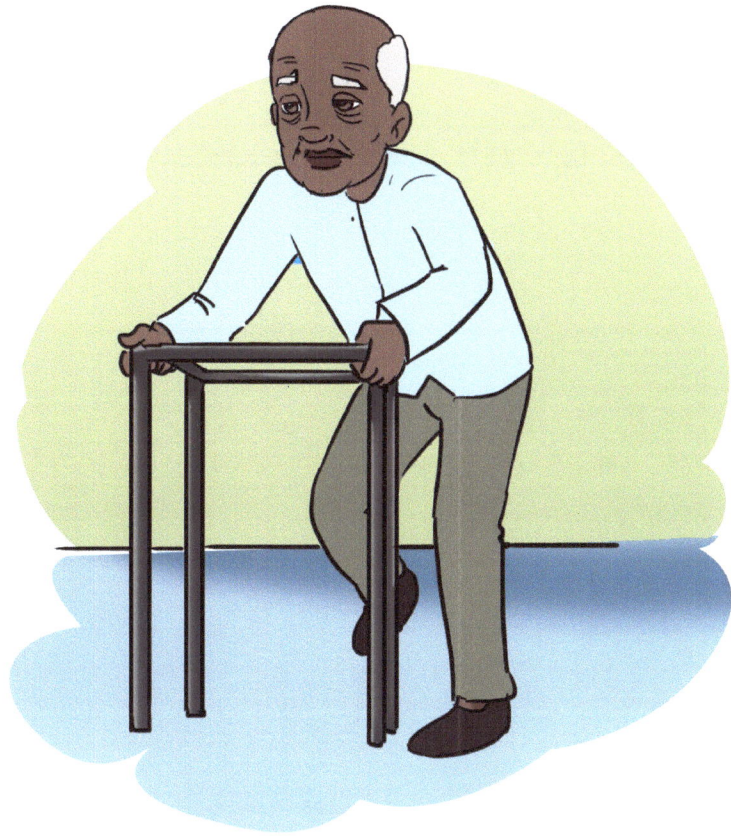

Every day, it didn't seem like Grandad was getting any better. He moved slower and slower until one day, Grandad couldn't get out of bed. This made Devin very sad. His parents were worried, and nurses came to visit Grandad every day.

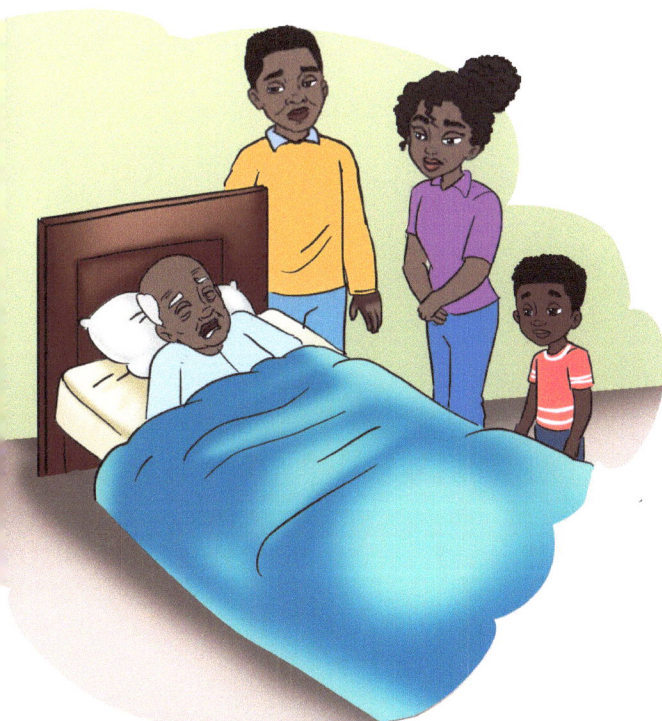

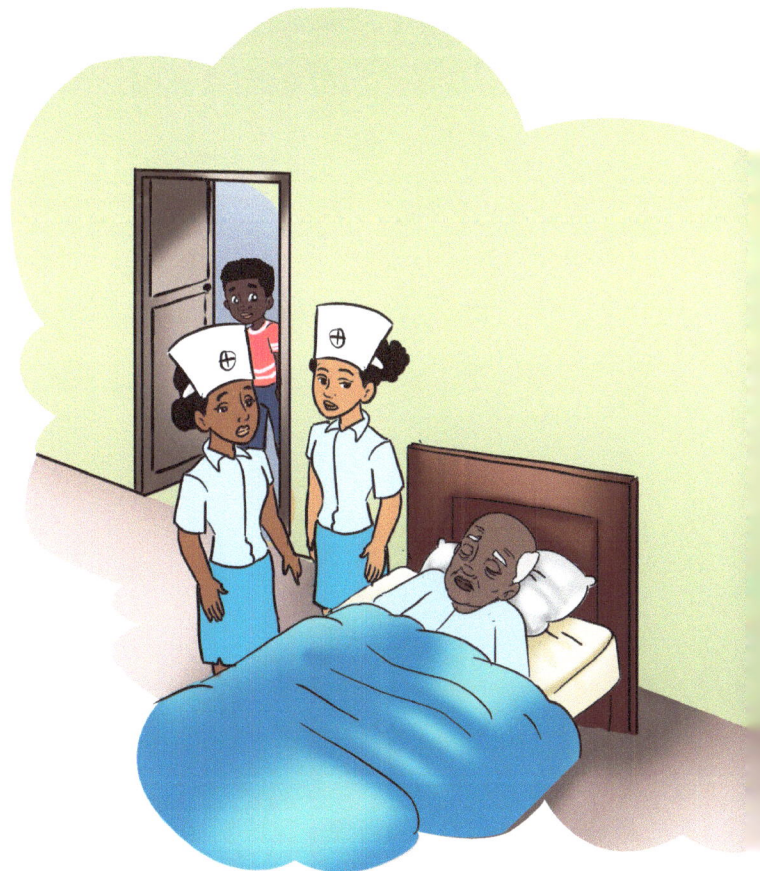

One cold winter day, Devin woke up and went to Grandad's room to see if he was feeling better. When Devin opened the door, his granddad was not there.

He searched all over the house. Grandad wasn't in the hall, the living room, the bathroom, or in the kitchen. There was no trace of him in the whole house.

Then, Devin had a thought! "Maybe Granddad is better and went to celebrate!" Devin wasn't sure how long his granddad would be gone, but he looked forward to seeing him soon.

Devin noticed that his parents were very quiet that day. They looked very sad. Devin remembered what his mom told him about up and down days, so he gave his parents some space and played quietly.

One morning, his mom woke him early and told him to get dressed. His Sunday church clothes were laid on his bed. "But it's Saturday. We never go to church on Saturday," Devin said to his mom, confused. His mom looked very sad, so Devin followed her instructions and dressed for church.

When he walked out of his room, Devin noticed many of his relatives were in the living room. Everyone had on church clothes. Devin wondered if they were having a fancy party for his granddad. He searched the house for Grandad, but couldn't find him. So, he asked his Dad.

"Are we having a surprise party for granddad?" Devin asked, puzzled.
Devin's question made Dad even sadder. Dad looked down and shook his head
no. "Come with me, son. Let's talk for a minute." Devin thought he was in
trouble. His head drooped as he followed his dad to his room.
"Devin, do you remember how sick Grandad was?" Dad asked.
"Yes, I remember," Devin replied sadly. "Then he just disappeared. I thought
he was feeling better and went to celebrate. But everyone looks so sad."
"Well, son. Grandad's body got really tired. One morning, he died. That
means he is no longer here with us physically. The good thing is, he's not sick
anymore." Dad told Devin.
"Well, where is he? Where did he go? Can I go see him?" Devin asked, excited
to hear that his grandad was feeling better.

"Devin, when people die, they go to a different place. It's a little hard to explain. When we go to the church, you will see Grandad's body, but it will be like he is asleep." Dad explained.

"Asleep? I thought you said he was feeling better?" Devin was confused.

Dad took a deep breath. "Do you remember how they talk about our spirit at church?" Devin nodded his head yes.

"Well, our spirit is what makes us who we are. Our spirits make our bodies alive. Everything you loved about your grandad was his spirit. His laugh, his funny jokes, and his cool ideas were Grandad's spirit. Our spirits never die. When our bodies get tired and die, our spirits leave our bodies and go to Heaven. In Heaven, God gives our spirit a new body. We don't have to use our old body anymore. We don't have to deal with the bad things that happen on Earth. We get to be in Heaven with God in our new bodies."

"So, I don't get to see Grandad in his new body? I don't get to see him ever again?" Devin asked.

"No, not right now. But one day, when it is your time to get a new body, you will see Grandad again." Dad explained.

"That is a really long time to wait, Dad. I'm really going to miss Grandad." Devin said sadly.

"I know, son. We all will. We are all happy that Grandad has a new body in heaven. But we are going to miss him on Earth. That's why everyone is so sad." Dad told Devin.

Devin didn't understand everything Dad said but understood that he wouldn't see Grandad anytime soon. Devin felt a lot of different things. He was happy Grandad was feeling better, but Devin was sad he wouldn't see Grandad.

In children's church, they always talked about how beautiful heaven was. Devin was happy Grandad was in a better place. But he wondered if Grandad had friends there. Devin wondered if his grandad liked heaven or if he felt alone. Devin also felt afraid. He wondered what it would be like when it was time for his body to die. Would it hurt? How would he get to heaven? Who would show him around? So many questions filled Devin's mind. Devin sat in his room and did not speak to anyone for the rest of the morning.

At Grandad's funeral that afternoon, Devin watched and listened as everyone spoke about his grandad. They talked about the man his granddad "was." Every time they said "was," Devin fidgeted in his seat. Even though Dad said Grandad's spirit didn't die, everyone kept talking about Grandad as if he didn't exist anymore. This made Devin mad. He stood up and stormed out of the funeral.

Devin was relieved when the funeral was over. When they got home, he went to his room, changed his clothes, and sat in the bed. Soon, his house filled with people. The adults ate and talked, and his cousins joined him in the living room. None of them talked. They all sat in silence. Devin heard the adults laughing and talking in the living room. He couldn't understand why they were suddenly happy. He was still very sad.

A few of Devin's relatives stayed at their house for the rest of the holiday break. His family made gingerbread houses, a scrapbook filled with pictures of Grandad, and even opened presents. Devin didn't enjoy any of their fun activities. He thought about Grandad every day.

When the holidays were over, Devin's relatives left. Some mornings, Devin would go to the guest room to see if Grandad had dropped in for a surprise visit. Each time, Devin was disappointed because Grandad wasn't there.

Devin was usually pretty happy about school, but things were different now that Grandad was gone. Devin met Savannah at the bus stop but did not speak. When she asked him how his winter break went, he only shrugged.

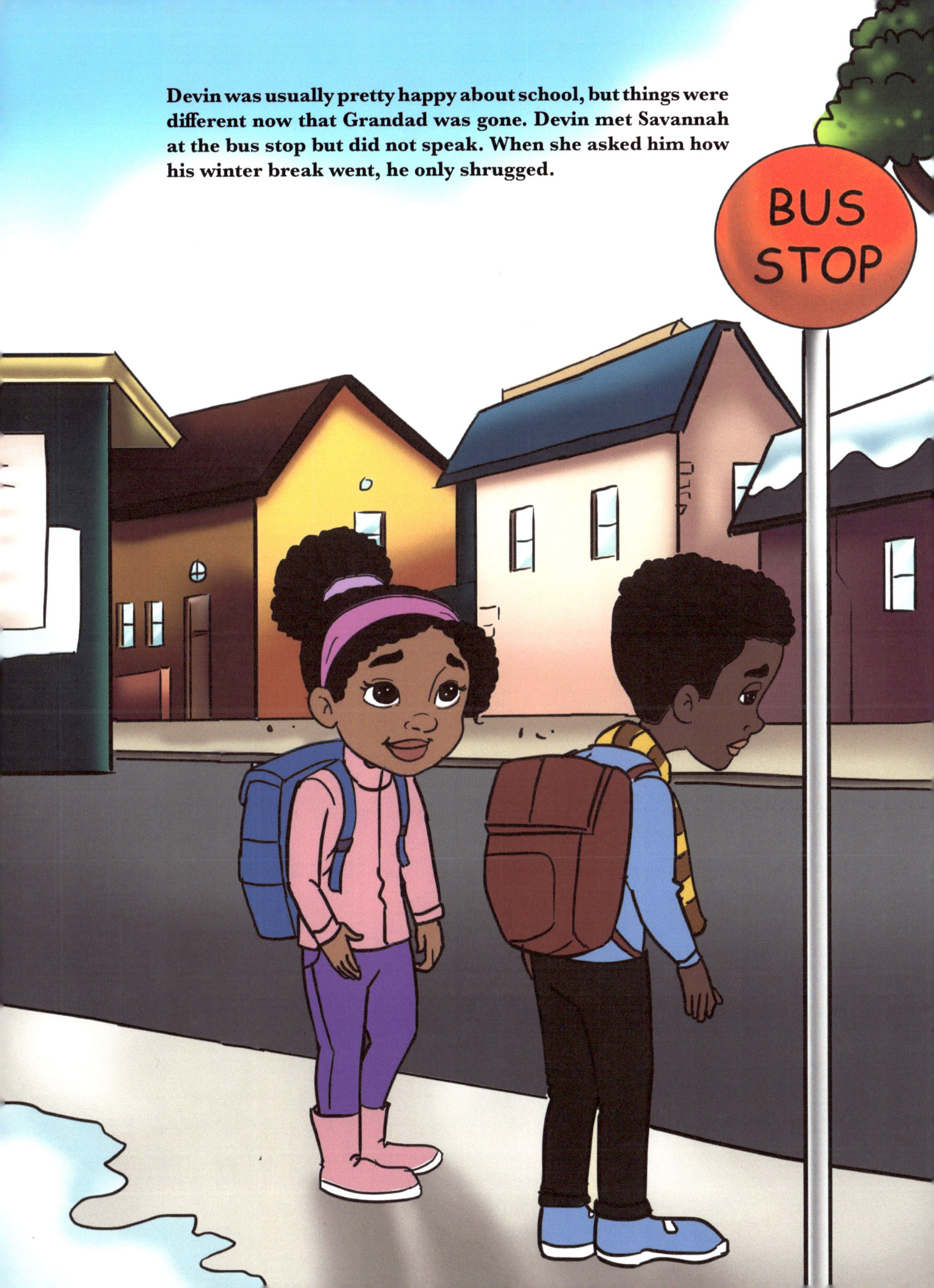

BUS STOP

When Devin got to school, he only felt worse. Everyone was laughing and having fun. Teachers were smiling and welcoming everyone back. Devin felt like no one cared that Grandad was gone.

Everyone was acting as if nothing had changed.
Devin couldn't understand any of it. He became
angry and could not wait to get back to his room.

After school, Devin stormed into the house and went straight to his room. When Mom heard his door slam, she went to his room to check on him.

"Are you okay, Devin? Did something happen at school?" Mom asked.

"NO! I am not okay! Everyone is acting normal, like nothing happened! But Grandad is gone! He's never coming back here! And I have to wait until I am very old to see him. That is not fair!" Devin shouted.

"Devin, everybody at school didn't know your Grandad. Everything is normal for them." Mom explained calmly.

"But that isn't fair! How does someone leave this Earth, and everyone keeps acting like nothing happened!" Devin shouted back.

Devin's mom didn't know what to say. Devin got in his bed and threw the covers over his head. He was angry at everyone and everything. He didn't want to talk. He stayed in his room until dinner time.

At dinner, Devin didn't eat. He stared at the seat where his Grandad would sit, and tears rolled down his face. Devin did not even want his favorite dessert. After dinner, he excused himself from the table and went to bed.

Devin's mom and dad did not know what to do to help him. After Devin went to bed, they talked and decided to get Devin a therapist to help him deal with his grief.

The next day, Devin walked to the bus stop with his head down. He could hear other kids talking and laughing. He could only frown at the sound of the kids playing. He wanted to speak up and tell everyone to stop, but he didn't say anything. He didn't respond to any "good morning" calls. He kept his head down and boarded the bus when it arrived.

"What's wrong?" Savannah asked Devin, sitting down beside him.
Bursting with emotions, Devin shared the news about his granddad with Savannah. "Everyone else is happy and smiling, but I feel awful! No one understands how hard it was for me! I can't see my grandad anymore!"

"I do. The same thing happened to me when my aunt died," Savannah shared quietly. Devin and Savannah stared at each other.

"Is that why you were sad for so many days?" Devin asked Savannah.
Savannah nodded. "It was hard because no one around me changed. My aunt was gone, and everyone acted like nothing happened. Everyone else stayed the same." Devin gasped. "That's exactly how I feel!" Devin exclaimed.

Devin and Savannah couldn't believe they were going through something similar. They talked about it the entire bus ride to school. Devin felt less alone the longer they talked, and so did Savannah.

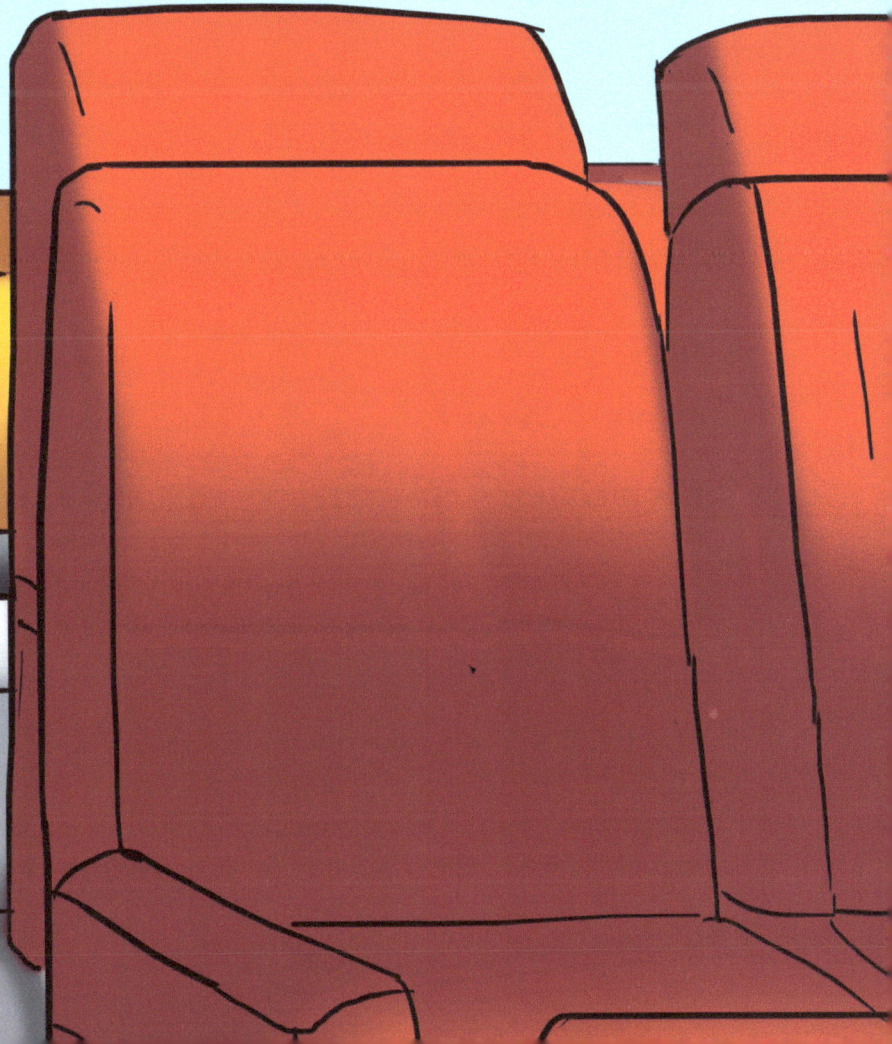

After school, Devin's parents took him to his first session with his therapist. Devin was very nervous at first, but talking to Savannah earlier made him more comfortable opening up about his feelings. Also, his therapist was very kind and understanding.

"Devin, I am here to help you talk through your feelings. It takes time to get over grief, but talking about it can help you feel better every day."

"Wow!" Devin said. "I thought that if I didn't talk about it, my feelings would eventually go away."

His therapist smiled. "You know, a lot of people feel that way. But anger and sadness don't go away if we don't talk about it. Those feelings stay in our hearts for a very long time. They can even make us mean or sick if we don't get those bad feelings out. It is never good to hold bad feelings inside. We have to find a healthy way to get them out."

"Like talking to a therapist or your friends?" Devin asked.

"Yep! You got it. There are different ways to get different feelings out. But talking and sharing is the best way to get sadness out of us."

Devin was thrilled about everything he learned in therapy. He couldn't wait to share it with Savannah. Now, when they were feeling sad about something, they shared their feelings with each other. Savannah and Devin grew even closer as friends. They knew that they could always talk to their parents and each other if they were having a hard time.

Devin continued to go to therapy and was feeling a lot better. As winter went away and the trees began to sprout new leaves, Devin thought about his grandad a lot. He didn't push away those thoughts. He smiled about all of the springtime memories he had with his grandad. Every spring, they would plant new things in the garden, go for walks in the park, and draw pictures of birds they saw at his grandad's house.

He shared those memories with Savannah. Savannah also shared memories of fun things she and her aunt did during the springtime.

As they walked home from school one day, Devin had a cool idea.
"What if we did those things together? We could go to the park and draw pictures of birds!"

"And we could plant flowers like my aunt and your grandad did in my backyard!" Savannah finished his sentence.

They shared their idea with their parents, and both families agreed to do the activities together. They had a lot of fun and shared memories of their loved ones as they enjoyed the activities together.

Even though losing his grandad was hard, Devin realized he was still surrounded by people who loved and cared for him.

Sometimes, Devin was sad that he couldn't see his grandad, but talking about his feelings and sharing happy memories with Savannah and his family made him feel better.

Grandad wasn't there with him physically anymore, but Devin knew Grandad's spirit would always be alive in his heart.

About the Author

Having developed a passion for reading at a young age, **Author Dwanetta Beaver Reed** dreamed of someday becoming a published author and writing children's books that promoted positive self-image and self-esteem. After Dwanetta's life took a devastating turn in 2018 when she and her husband lost their seven-year-old daughter, Katherine, she chose a different direction for her first publications. The challenge of comforting their son as he grappled with the loss of his older sister inspired Dwanetta to dedicate her first books to helping children navigate the challenges of grief and loss.

A devout Christian, Dwanetta considers her faith in and love for Jesus Christ the foundation of her life. She enjoys serving the community and volunteering as a youth leader at her church. Dwanetta is passionate about positively impacting the next generation and aims to make a difference in the lives of youth through every encounter she is granted.

By trade, Dwanetta is a systems engineer, having obtained a Bachelor's in Electrical Engineering from Tennessee State University and a Master's in Systems Engineering from the University of Alabama in Huntsville. However, she considers her most significant accomplishments being a wife, mother, daughter, sister, aunt, cousin, and friend. Family and friends mean the world to Dwanetta, and she loves spending time with her loved ones, traveling, doing fun and new activities, and making lasting memories.

Dwanetta wholeheartedly believes in being supportive, a great listener, and valuing relationships over monetary things. She hopes to instill these qualities in youth worldwide through books and other endeavors.

INSTAGRAM   @dwanetta51
FACEBOOK   Dwanetta Reed

www.ingramcontent.com/pod-product-compliance
Lightning Source LLC
Chambersburg PA
CBHW060812090426

42737CB00002B/43